I0675986

Changing
Seasons 2
A New Leaf

Written By: Laura Hansen
Cover Model: Audree Adams

Chapter 1

While everyone thought that Jordan was LeAnn's guardian angel, Alex believed something different. He felt that she was watching over everyone. LeAnn said that Jordan visits her in her dreams. No one knows, but Jordan visits him too.

While everyone was busy cleaning up after the party, Alex helped LeAnn put away her new toys in her bedroom. Her three-year old sister was taking a nap, and her older brother was in his bedroom playing video games.

He asked her about the dreams she's been having about Jordan. "She's not going to visit me anymore." LeAnn said. "Oh. Why?" Alex asked. "I'm not supposed to tell anyone." LeAnn whispered. "I'm good at keeping secrets." Alex whispered back.

"She's a new person." LeAnn whispered. "Really. Who is she now?" Alex played along. "I've said too much. I can't say anymore." LeAnn stated.

Just then Brit came into the room. "LeAnn come say goodbye to grandma and grandpa." She ordered. "I should probably get going too." Alex added. LeAnn gave him a big hug. "Bye Alex." LeAnn said.

A part of Alex wanted to believe LeAnn, but a five-year old can have quite the imagination. He believed in Heaven and

God, but now he wondered, "Would God reincarnate someone?" After all God is powerful and could do anything. Then another part of him thought that reincarnation was just a fairy tale. A way of people wishing their loved ones would come back.

But he found it coincidental that he too was having dreams of Jordan. LeAnn had never met Jordan and she seemed to know exactly who she was, but he's sure her family has talked about her often. His grief made it hard to move on. A part of him felt it was the reason for all his dreams, but what was LeAnn's reason?

He believes that everything happens for a reason... but reincarnation? Would God rebirth a soul into another body? Would she get a second chance at life?

"LeAnn said she's a new person. Does that mean she's already been reborn? If so, then why do I still feel her presence all around me?" He wondered. He shook his head at himself. "This is crazy talk" He thought.

He would dream about her every night. Her beautiful blue eyes gazing up at him. He was weak for those eyes. The touch of her soft and silky lips against his. The sweet smell of her shampoo as the breeze blew across her hair. There were so many things he missed about her. It's been seven years since she passed away, but for Alex it still felt like yesterday.

His dreams always started out the same. It would always start out good. So good. They'd be holding one another and gazing into each other's eyes. "I've missed you." He whispered as he ran his fingers through her hair and down her back. He gently kissed her silky lips.

She looked so good in her silky petal pink gown. She looked like an angel... but she didn't kiss like an angel. An angels kiss would be innocent and gentle. She kissed him as if it was the last time she would ever kiss him. It was passionate and full of desire.

He could feel the excitement underneath his pants. She could feel it too, which only led to more heavy kissing. The more passionate it got, the more the earth began to shake. The ground split between them. It was as if the universe was trying to separate them and forbidding them to be together.

They reached their hands out for one another, but they were too far apart. So, he took a running leap. The hole in the earth was too big. He fell into the empty black hole. That's when he would wake up drenched in tears and sweat. His desire turned into heartache, and it repeated itself every night. He missed her. He would never get over her. He only longed for her.

His dreams always felt so real. You know that feeling you get that you're really falling in your sleep? That's what it felt like. Like he really fell into that black hole and landed in his bed.

He had this feeling that she never left him. As if she visited him every night but could never stay.

He was only twenty-four when she passed away. He knew he had to move on eventually. He was thirty-one years old and all his friends had families now. He was still a single bachelor. A very sexy bachelor. Most of the single women at the hospital wanted to date him. They were turned on by his good looks and muscular body. He had very good genetics. They would flirt continuously. He would innocently flirt back, but never took any of the women home. Besides, he had Jordan to look forward to in his dreams every night.

He tried to stay busy outside of work. He would meet Blake at the gym several times a week. He tried to take his mind off Jordan. He wasn't ready to let her go. He felt that he would never be ready. She was the love of his life.

He hadn't moved on since her death. He couldn't imagine himself with anyone else. She was his soul mate and no one could ever compare. He would never love anyone the way he loved her. As far as he was concerned, he would die alone.

He felt a great responsibility to look after Jordan's family. She always wanted them to be okay after she was gone. As the years went on, it was getting harder and harder to be around them. Everything about them reminded him of Jordan. So much that it hurt.

For the most part everyone was okay. He could still tell the pain was still there. They would get silent every time something reminded them of Jordan, or when they enjoyed something she would have enjoyed. Holidays were always hard on them. They still left an empty chair at the dinner table where she used to sit. They would always miss her.

As he saw Taylor and LeAnn grow up, he noticed how much Taylor resembled Jordan. Even down to her personality. He started to come around less and less.

He stopped having dreams of Jordan, and he would never forget the last dream he had of her. It was a couple weeks after LeAnn's fifth birthday party.

It started out as it always did, but something was different about this dream. This time she was in a red lace lingerie. She was gentle with her kiss and gentle with her touch. They were lying in bed in front of a warm fireplace. Her cheeks were flushed. They held each other underneath the covers, bodies pressed up against one another. He had nothing on under the covers.

The earthquake never came. They made love to each other. This felt so real. A dream that he never wanted to wake up from. It was the only piece of her that he had left. Seeing her beautiful face every night. He dreaded the morning when she would disappear.

As the dream came to an end, she whispered softly, "I'll find you. Recognize me Alex."

Her voice echoed as he awoke from his dream. "Recognize me." This dream stood out from the rest. He couldn't make sense of it. He knew he longed for her and wanted her back. But apart of him wondered, "Is she trying to tell me something?" He wanted to believe that it was possible that she would come back.

He wondered, "Is this just a dream of his subconscious thoughts, or could it in fact be possible that she is being reincarnated?"

Chapter 2
(15 years later)

Blake and Brit were sending out invites to Taylor's eighteenth birthday party. Her older sister LeAnn was putting gold glittery stars in each envelope.

"What am I turning five LeAnn? What's with the glittery stars?" Taylor laughed. "You were born June 18th. You're turning eighteen which makes this your "star birthday" or as some would say your golden birthday." LeAnn explained. Taylor giggled, "Whatever you say."

Taylor loved how thoughtful she was. She was such an amazing sister. "You're lucky. My star birthday was when I was seven. At least you're older and can choose your fun." LeAnn stated.

"I'm surprised you didn't want to do a fancy evening ball with pretty gowns for your birthday like your sister did. We have the club house that has a balcony with stairs leading into the ball room for you to walk down." Brit said.

"Maybe for my future wedding." Taylor joked. She wasn't like her sister, and she was so grateful that Alex was letting her have her birthday party at his cancer hospital. Her invites asked people to donate to the cancer center and to bring gift baskets to give to the sick patients rather than buying her a birthday present.

She wanted to give to people who were suffering. She wanted to bring them some joy during their difficult journey. She knew what it was like to suffer. She had everything she wanted except one thing... for Alex to know who she was. She wanted so badly to work up the courage to tell him that she is Jordan. That she had been reborn.

She knew how complicated this would be, since she had been reborn as her brother's daughter. She knew she had a rough road ahead if she chose to tell him who she was. She knew their love would never be accepted. She knew that their love would be forbidden.

She often wondered if he still loved her. She knew that he still loved her fifteen years ago. She remembers his dreams, she was there with him in his dreams. Although she was three years old at the time, she had the same dreams.

She had a choice to make. To live her life out as Taylor and find a new love and pretend that she never lived a previous life, and never tell Alex, or complicate everything for the sake of love by telling him who she is, even if it's forbidden, and the chance that he might not even believe her.

The thought of it made her heart race and her palms sweat. "What if he believed me? What if we fought for our love and eventually everyone accepted it? What if it would be worth the fight? Sometimes the things that are so precious is worth a fight. The best things never come easy." She thought.

Just then she got a great idea. "What if I gave him a hint as to who I am?" She thought. She could make cards with a falling leaf on it and write "Life is like a changing season" This was a quote that Alex had told her when she battled cancer when she lived as Jordan. He gave her a falling leaf necklace for her birthday.

She would also send him a thank you card for letting her have her party at his hospital and put the same quote and falling leaf symbol in his card. Hopefully he would catch on.

Chapter 3

Her birthday turned out exactly how she pictured it. She brought a moment of happiness to all the patients at the hospital.

"Those cards you did was a nice touch. It was a very neat idea. Where did you get an idea like that?" LeAnn asked. "It was what Alex told me on my birthday when he had given me a falling leaf necklace. I didn't want to celebrate my birthday because I was dying and felt no reason to celebrate a life I wasn't going to live. He helped me through it." Taylor explained.

"When are you going to tell him who you are?" LeAnn asked. "I'm hoping these cards did." Taylor stated. "Men don't usually catch on to subtle hints. What are you waiting for?" LeAnn asked. Taylor took a deep nervous breath, "What if he doesn't believe me?" She asked. "What if he does?" LeAnn asked.

Her heart raced at the idea of telling him. "How would I say it?" She wondered. She couldn't just blurt it out. "What if he thought I was crazy?" She wondered. She would hate for him to think that she was playing a joke on him. She wouldn't want to see him hurt.

LeAnn has known her whole life. Jordan told her in a dream before Taylor was ever born. This bonded them as sisters. It made them closer than ever. LeAnn has kept this secret her whole life.

She wanted to tell Alex in his dreams, in a way she did. She told him that she'd find him. She told him to try to recognize her. So, she was hoping he would catch on to her subtle hints.

At the end of the night, Taylor said goodnight to all her guests. "We'll see you at home in the morning." Blake said. "Happy birthday sweet heart." Brit said. "You girls behave." Blake joked as he and Brit left the hospital. LeAnn was going to take her out for a little after party. "I'll go get the car." LeAnn said leaving her alone with Alex.

"Thank you for all of this. You put a smile on all their faces. It was truly a nice gesture." Alex said. "Thank you for letting me do it." She replied. He wondered about the cards she gave everyone, including the thank you card she gave him. He remembered that quote like it was yesterday, and the falling leaf. Memories he had kept close to his heart. Then he remembered that Blake had a falling leaf key chain that Jordan gave him before she died. "That must have been where she got the idea." He thought.

"Can I ask you something?" Taylor asked. "Sure." He replied. "Do you believe that God does everything for a reason?" She asked. "I do. I believe he has a purpose for everything."

"What about reincarn…" Taylor began to say before she was interrupted. "You ready?" LeAnn yelled as she walked through the hospital doors.

"Have fun. Happy birthday." Alex said. "Thank you." She replied.

"I was just about to tell him." Taylor said when they got in the car. "Well go back in there." LeAnn insisted. "I can't, it's too late, the moment is gone." She said.

"I honestly don't even know what I would have said. I probably would've chickened out. Even if he did believe me, there would be no future for us. No one would approve." Taylor explained.

She was Blakes little girl now. She wasn't his sister anymore. He would never believe that she was reincarnated. This wasn't fair. A part of her felt this was life's cruel joke. First, she dies from cancer. Now she's reincarnated and can't be with the man she loves.

She put her problems aside for the night and had an amazing time with her sister and friends at the party LeAnn put together.

Taylor had two best friends. Alison and Jack. They weren't the type of friends she would have chosen in her past life. Most of her past life she only associated herself with people who came from money. She used to be all about her reputation and status was everything.

She was naïve. She changed for the better. Her friends Alison and Jack didn't have rich families. They didn't have a college fund aside for them. They had to work to save for college. Taylor and Alison both worked as housekeepers at the hotel at her family's golf resort. Occasionally Taylor would help at the front desk. Everyone thought she was a fast learner. Little did they know that she had done all of this before. Jack worked there also, he worked at the counter where he'd check people in at the hotel.

Taylor was unsure who she wanted to be, but one thing she loved was art. She loved paintings that resembled an emotion rather than a place. She loved the paintings that most people would question what the picture was.

Alison had dreams of being a news reporter. When ever they'd clean a hotel room she always put the television on the news channel and would listen to it as she cleaned. Most teenagers would put a music channel and jam to the music. Taylor loved how different she was to your everyday normal teenager.

Jack wanted to be a photographer. He loved pictures. "The best pictures are the ones you don't pose for." Jack would always say. They were moments captured in time. Taylor agreed to let Jack take photos of her to go with his college applications. He was very talented in his work, and she'd do anything for her friends.

Although Taylor was unsure what she wanted to do with her life, one thing was for sure. She wanted to be with Alex. She wanted to see the world. Especially New York at Christmas time. Nothing was going to hold her back. She knew that life was short. She wanted to experience so many things and chase after dreams.

She wanted everyone to know who she was but feared that no one would believe her. The only proof she had was memories and the dreams she shared with LeAnn and Alex. She was disappointed that Alex didn't catch on to her subtle hints. He hasn't come around as much as he used to.

After Jordan died he came around all the time, but ever since LeAnn's fifth birthday, he started coming around less and less. He and Blake would work out together at the gym a couple times a week, but that was it.

The morning after her party LeAnn woke Taylor up early. "What are you doing up so early?" Taylor asked. "I couldn't sleep. I've been thinking, maybe you should just blurt out who you are to Alex. Maybe that's the only way." LeAnn suggested.

"He will think I'm crazy." Taylor mumbled. "You got a second chance at life. There's got to be a reason you came back. To give you and Alex a real chance at love and happiness." LeAnn said.

"You don't understand. It's not that simple." Taylor argued. "I may not know what it's like in your shoes, but I can see that it is hurting you that he doesn't know. I think you would feel so much better if it was out in the open. Even if he didn't believe you at first. I think you just need him to know." LeAnn said.

LeAnn wanted to help her sister. She had been keeping this secret for too long. It was time that she told Alex who she really was.

Chapter 4

LeAnn remembered her dreams of Jordan as if they were yesterday. She remembered Jordan telling her that she was going to be her sister. She was reborn into Taylor. She remembered Jordan making her promise that she would never tell, and that this secret would bond them forever.

She was right. They had a special bond, but with that special bond also came with a heavy burden. A secret that she must never tell. It wasn't fair for Jordan to ask her to keep such a juicy secret.

She has kept her secret her whole life. Now that Taylor is eighteen and officially an adult who can make her own choices, LeAnn felt that it was time that she came out with it. Nothing should hold her back. She needs to tell Alex who she is.

She often wondered if the reason Alex hadn't been around much in the last fifteen years, is because of the last thing she said to him. Alex knew she was having dreams of Jordan. Periodically they would see him, and Taylor resembled Jordan so much. She wondered if it was hard for Alex to look at her because she looked so much like Jordan.

"If he only knew." LeAnn thought to herself. It's not only Alex that she wanted to know. She wanted the whole family to know. She wanted her grandparents to know that they had their daughter back. She wanted Blake to know he had his sister back. Then they all wouldn't feel the pain of Jordan being gone anymore. Even though it's been years, she knew the heartache was still there.

How could they get everyone to believe it? This doesn't seem like something that would happen in real life. This was magical. This was a gift. Jordan died young and she deserved a second chance.

Alex is a giving soul. He devoted his life to taking care of sick people. If anyone deserved to be happy it was him. He's never loved anyone but Jordan. He never got married or had kids. He just put his heart and soul into his work. He felt closer to Jordan with each cancer patient. He deserved this second chance. Even if they're years apart now. It's still her and age didn't matter. Age is just a number. Her body may be eighteen, but her soul was the same age as he is.

Taylor often visited Susan and Jacob. She too wished that she could tell everyone who she was. Whenever she hugged them she would hug them extra tight.

She often worried about her future. Hoping and praying that she wouldn't end up with cancer again. She couldn't take the pain of leaving her family twice, and she didn't think they could handle another loss.

"Would it even be fair to them if she told them who she really was?" She wondered as she put her cleaning cart away. They loved Taylor too and she wasn't sure she could take that away from them. It took them years to cope with Jordan being gone.

As she walked out of the supply closet, she noticed a familiar face checking into the hotel. One person she thought she would never see again was in town for the summer for a golf tournament. Joshua Haze, her cheating ex. He had a son who was LeAnn's age. His son was in the tournament as well. Cameron Haze. Taylor had noticed LeAnn checking him out as she was checking them into the hotel. She seemed to be flirting with Cameron.

She wondered if she should pull her aside and warn her about them. If Cameron was anything like his father, LeAnn would end up heartbroken.

Joshua Haze took notice in Taylor. She looked so much like Jordan. If he's anything like he was in the past, she knew he was trouble. He loved women and money.

Her friend Jack was working that day, and he helped them with their luggage to their hotel rooms. Joshua whispered to his assistant "You think at my age I could still get one that young?" He asked as he looked at Taylor. "With your reputation, I don't see why not. Girls love to be wined and dined." He replied.

"The best part is my wife doesn't come on tours with me, and my son has a separate hotel room." Joshua thought to himself. He was determined to have her before the end of the summer. "Even if I have to slip a little something in her drink." He thought to himself.

Chapter 5

Taylor couldn't stop thinking about Alex. It was driving her crazy. She wanted to tell him who she was, but still had no idea how to bring it up. She was afraid that he wouldn't believe her and that she'd end up looking like a fool... but that was her fear talking. Her heart was saying that he would believe her. He had always had faith in the unknown. He taught her so much about faith. Believing in things that were unseen and having faith in what seemed impossible.

She had to tell him. She couldn't hold it inside anymore. "I'll tell him tonight." She thought to herself as she looked at her reflection in the bathroom mirror at the hotel.

Her family was having a welcoming party for all the golfers. Alex was invited just because he was Blakes close friend.

"You look nervous." LeAnn said as she walked into the bathroom. "I'm going to tell Alex who I am tonight." Taylor said. "Finally!" LeAnn exclaimed. "Shh. I don't want anyone to hear us." Taylor whispered. "Finally." LeAnn whispered. Taylor rolled her eyes at LeAnn's sense of humor.

"Need my help?" LeAnn asked. "No. I'm nervous enough as it is." Taylor said. "Good, cause I'm Cameron Haze's date tonight for the welcoming party." LeAnn said.

"Ugh, don't fall for an egotistical golfer." Taylor warned. "He's not like the other golfers, don't worry. Besides, he's so hot." LeAnn blushed.

Taylor wanted to tell her that she used to be engaged to Cameron's father. But seeing how excited and hopeful she was made it difficult. She was young and desiring to experience her own life. She couldn't fix her mistakes through LeAnn. She knew she'd have to pick up the broken pieces if he hurt her. She knew she would have to pay very close attention to Cameron.

If anything, she would have to warn her about Cameron's family and what she could be getting herself into. Especially if things were to get serious.

The party was packed full of people. The club house had a ball room with crystal chandeliers. There were waiters serving glasses of champagne.

Taylor was wearing a beautiful white pearl silk gown. Her hair was pulled back in a bun with pearl clips on the side of her head, and a string of pearls around her neck.

Her older sister wore a black sparkly gown and left her hair down. They were both beautiful and caught the eyes of many men in the room. LeAnn brought Cameron as her date. It was the kind of party where everyone wore evening gowns and black tuxedo's.

A quarter way through the party, Taylor heard a loud crash! A waiter dropped a tray of champagne. "I'll go get some towels." Taylor insisted. She wanted tonight to be perfect for her parents. They do this event every year for the golfers. It was important that everyone had a great time. After all, word of mouth was the best advertising for their company.

She went into the linen closet and was shocked to see LeAnn and Cameron making out. Her dress was unzipped and so were his pants. It looked as if they were doing some heavy touching and about to take making out to the next step.

"Oh my gosh!" Taylor yelled as they hurried to zip up their clothing. "What are you doing?" LeAnn exclaimed. "I need towels." Taylor said as she covered her eyes as she held her hand out waiting for them to put them in her hand.

Taylor quickly stormed out of the closet and brought them to the waiter. She then stormed out on to the balcony. "This can't be happening!" She thought to herself. "LeAnn cannot fall for him." She whispered to herself.

"Everything okay?" A familiar voice behind her said. She turned around and saw Joshua Haze standing behind her. Even in his middle age he was still a good-looking man, but she knew what type of guy he was. He was manipulative and shady. "I'm fine." She said hoping that he would just leave.

"You look like you could use a drink." He said as he handed her his glass of champagne. "I'm not old enough. I'm only eighteen." She replied hoping he'd see that she is too young for him. "Well, then I guess it'll just have to be our little secret." Joshua said.

She wasn't sure what else to say. He seemed so persistent. So, she took the glass. "Don't worry, I'll keep a look out. If anyone sees, I'll just say you were holding it a second for me." He assured her.

She was feeling so stressed out. "What would one glass of champagne do?" She thought to herself as she chugged the whole glass.

Chapter 6

Taylor awoke in someone else's bed. "Where am I and how did I get here?" She thought to herself. She looked under the covers and saw that she was still in her evening dress. "I only remember drinking one glass of champagne." She thought. "You're awake." Alex said from the door way.

"Why am I here?" She asked.

"You seemed to have had a lot to drink last night. LeAnn was persistent about you spending the night here. Last night was a big night for your dad. I normally don't try to cover up a teenager's drunk escapade, but I know how important last night was for your dad and the family business. LeAnn said she left a note that you stayed the night at your girlfriend's house."

Taylor wasn't surprised. Especially after catching LeAnn and Cameron in the closet together. "Now she has something against me, so I can't snitch her out." Taylor thought. What bothered her more was that she only had one glass of champagne. How could she have blocked out the whole night?

"I only had one glass of champagne." Taylor admitted. "It didn't look like that was all you had. You were passing out drunk, how did you even get a glass of champagne? I know they ask for identification." Alex said.

"Joshua Haze." Taylor admitted. The name made Alex's blood boil. His concerned expression quickly turned angered. "You need to stay away from him." He ordered.

Taylor had never seen him so angry. The Alex she knew was sweet and attentive. This Alex was protective... and she liked it. "I wonder if he slipped something in your drink." Alex said.

"There's more." Taylor said as she began to cry. Alex was very concerned. "Did he hurt you?" He asked. Taylor took a deep breath as she wiped away her tears. "Not in this life." She cried.

"What do you mean?" Alex asked as he felt very confused by her comment. "I've lived this life before... as Jordan. I don't know why I'm here. Living a life as someone else... and why I remember everything about my past life." Taylor cried.

Alex started to feel uncomfortable and confused at the same time. He remembered the last dream he had of Jordan, when she told him to "recognize her". Could this be true? "Is this a cruel joke?" He asked.

"It's not a joke. I remember everything. Including the dreams of yours. I was in them. The re-occurring earthquake, but the last dream the earthquake never came. Those memories are real." She explained.

Alex was in complete shock! "I never told anyone about my dreams." He said. "I was there." Taylor said breathlessly.

Alex took a deep breath. "This is a lot to take in." He said. He believed her. There's no other way she could have known about the dreams. This didn't sound like something that would happen in real life.

"I was in LeAnn's dreams too. She's the only one who knows... besides you." Taylor said. "Why are we the only ones who get to know?" Alex asked. "I want everyone to know, but I don't think the rest of my family would believe me." Taylor said.

She knew she visited Blake in his dream when he was in a coma, but she still wasn't sure he'd believe her. Maybe if she came back as someone else and not his daughter. "Why haven't you moved on? You never got married or had a family of your own?" She asked.

"I spent my life trying to heal sick people. I dedicated my life to that. There wasn't room for anyone or anything else." He explained. Alex started to get choked up. "This is a lot to take in, and it's very confusing. I need time to sort this out." He said.

"I understand." Taylor said as she slipped on her shoes. "I'll give you a ride home." Alex offered.

Chapter 7

Taylor hadn't heard from Alex all week. She proved to him who she was. She was in fact Jordan. She was in his dreams. She remembered those dreams like they were yesterday. She thought he might still be in shock. It's not every day your dead girlfriend comes back to life as someone else. This is more than just complicated. It's emotionally confusing.

Not only was this going to be a hard thing to wrap their head around, there was the fear that they may never be able to be together. Their love would be frowned upon and downright forbidden.

Taylor couldn't take the silence anymore. They eventually needed to talk. They couldn't avoid this forever. She was unsure how much time to give him to let this all sink in. This kind of thing is unheard of.

"Have you heard from Alex yet?" LeAnn asked as she peaked her head in the doorway of Taylors room. "No, not yet." Taylor replied. LeAnn walked in and sat down on Taylors bed. "At least he knows now." LeAnn assured. "Yeah, I'm just not sure how much time I'm supposed to give him to think." Taylor said.

"Just put on something sexy, drive over there, and have a little make out session. That's the best way to break a mans silence." LeAnn joked.

"Is that what you do with Cameron?" Taylor joked back. LeAnn laughed. "I wish it were that easy." Taylor continued. "Your situation is complicated... Alex is hot too. I don't know what you're waiting for." LeAnn said.

"What has gotten into you? All you think about is making out with a hot guy." Taylor laughed.

"Every time Cameron and I make out, we get closer and closer to... you know." LeAnn hinted.

"Sex? Yeah, I saw that in the closet." Taylor said. "He's so patient with me. There's no rush. We're just having fun with what we're doing." LeAnn said.

"Fun can get you into trouble. I wish you would be careful with him." Taylor warned.

"Okay, now that's my Aunt talking. Can you just be my sister for a few minutes?" LeAnn said.

"Sorry, I just don't want to see you get hurt. That's all. Those pro golfers can be really into themselves." Taylor said from experience.

"You know, you're right. I should just go over to Alex's house and talk to him." Taylor said. She made up her mind that

that is what she is going to do. They have to talk. They can't stay silent forever.

Later that evening she told Blake and Brit that she was going to stay the night at Alison's house. She was hoping that her and Alex's talk would last all night. "What's one more lie?" She thought. As far as she was concerned her whole life was a lie.

She called her friend Alison on the way. "Hey, if my parents call to check in, can you just say I'm in the bathroom and can't come to the phone? I told them I was staying the night." Taylor explained.

"Where are you really going? Did you meet a guy? You met a guy, didn't you?" Alison joked. "Sort of." Taylor blushed. "Anyone I know?" Alison asked. "No. No one you know." Taylor lied.

Alison has been her best friend most of her life. She's met Alex a few times. But this is a secret that she can never tell. Not even her best friend.

Once she got to Alex's, she started to re-think this whole idea. She couldn't go back home. She couldn't even go to Alison's. She would bombard her with questions that she isn't ready to answer. She sat in her car for a few minutes gathering her thoughts, and what she was going to say when he opened the door. Her mind drew a complete blank. All she could feel was her nerves setting in.

As she got out of the car and walked up to the door, her heart pounded faster and faster. Her palms were sweaty as she rang the door-bell. She found it hard to catch her breath. Her nerves were completely taking over her body.

When he opened the door, her whole body froze. "Come in." He said quietly. Her legs felt shaky as she walked inside. "It's been a week. I was afraid you'd never talk to me again." She admitted.

"Never. I'm sorry I took so long. This is a lot to take in, and it still doesn't seem real." He replied. "So, you don't believe me?" She asked. "No, I believe you. I always dreamed that you could be here with me, cancer free. I never expected this. This doesn't seem possible. This is the kind of thing that only happens in movies. Not real life. I never got over you and now you're here... But you're someone else. It's very confusing." He explained.

"I know. It's taken me practically my whole life to adjust to this and it's still difficult. I want so badly for my brother to know I'm back and my parents." She cried.

She could see so much pain in his eyes. She was hurting too. She wished that things could have been different, but they're not. This is what they get.

"How is this going to work? You're Blake's little girl now. You're not his sister anymore. He would kill me if he found out there was romantic feeling between us." He confessed.

"I don't know. I guess we can only be friends in this life. I don't know how it could work... But I am still in love with you. That'll never change." She said as tears streamed down her face. Alex wiped her tears away and held her close. It hurt her so much to be in his arms. She wanted him more than words can explain.

"I should go." She whispered. There was no point in staying and making things more complicated than what they were. "Don't go. How long can you be out?" He asked. "All night. I told Blake I was staying the night at a friend's house." She replied.

"Then stay. You wouldn't want him asking why you're home early." He said. "Are you sure this is the best idea?" She asked. "I just want more time with you." He confessed.

They talked for hours about their past. The more they talked, the more real this became. It was like they picked up right where they left off... as if she never left. When he heard her laugh, she sounded just like Jordan. She still had the same laugh. Her body language was the same. The way she would run her fingers through her hair to keep it out of her face was the same.

He couldn't help but to lean in and kiss her. She kissed the same. Their kiss brought back memories of their first kiss. He placed his hand upon her face and kissed her again.

She too couldn't help herself. She missed him. She wanted him. As they continued to kiss, her hands made their way down to his belt buckle. Just then he hesitated. "This is forbidden. Blake would kill me if he ever found out." He thought.

"It's okay." Taylor said. He looked into her eyes. He even saw Jordan in her eyes. He couldn't tell her no. He loved her. He wanted her. His heart ached for her. He leaned in and began kissing her again as they removed each other's clothing.

Chapter 8

LeAnn noticed a change in Taylor over the next few days. She was glowing. She seemed so much happier. It's the same look LeAnn had when she first started dating Cameron. "You seem to be beaming these last few days. Did you and Alex finally talk?" LeAnn asked.

Taylor looked at LeAnn through the mirror with a smile on her face as she combed her hair. "We talked." Taylor replied. "And? Does he believe you?" LeAnn asked.

"He believes me. We talked for hours about our memories... Then, one thing led to another." Taylor confessed. She couldn't hold it in. She had to tell someone and LeAnn was the only other person who knew who she really was.

"What! My younger sister lost her virginity before I did!" LeAnn exclaimed. She was a bit jealous. She was older. She's supposed to experience everything first. She's the one who's supposed to be giving advice to her younger sister about this stuff.

"It's not like it was really my first time. I've had sex in my past life." Taylor reminded her. "Sorry. I keep forgetting. It's just I still think of you as my little sister. This whole reincarnation thing is quite confusing. It's almost like I don't know which one you are to me. My Aunt Jordan or my younger sister Taylor." LeAnn explained.

Taylor felt bad. LeAnn has had to carry this deep secret her whole life, she could imagine what a burden it must be. If she would have known this would hurt her so much, she never would have visited her in her dreams.

She just wanted everyone to know who she really was. She wanted everyone to know that she was in fact Jordan. But maybe that's not who she's supposed to be anymore. She was given a second chance. She's supposed to experience a new life as Taylor. How can she do that when all she's ever known her true self to be is Jordan? There must be a reason for this.

"I am so sorry that you've had to keep this secret all these years. It wasn't fair for me to do that to you." Taylor apologized.

LeAnn began to cry. "I'm glad you told me. I just wish that everyone else knew so that this could feel normal... I know a part of you that no one else does. But at the same time, I want you to be my sister." LeAnn explained.

"I am your sister." Taylor assured her. LeAnn laughed, "Yeah, and you're my Aunt Jordan too. You can't change that." LeAnn said.

It was hard for Taylor to accept the fact that Jordan is dead, and Taylor is very much alive. She didn't know how to accept her new role in life, and why it happened. It wasn't fair.

Why couldn't she have just beaten the cancer and carry on with her old life.

Later that day she visited Jordan's grave. "Why did you have to go and die? You screwed everything up for us!" Taylor cried. It was so hard to feel like you were two people, or a soul trapped in someone else's body. She was holding on so tight to her past life that she couldn't exist as Taylor. It was like she was living a double life.

She didn't want Alex to feel this burden too. She feared this burden would eventually kill his romantic feelings for her. There were too many secrets, and with secrets would come resentment. It wasn't fair for the ones she loved to carry this heavy burden.

"I can't change who I am." Taylor whispered as she glared at her grave. She wasn't sure how much longer she could keep this a secret. Eventually the secret would come out. It weighed so heavy on her heart.

Poor LeAnn. So young. She shouldn't have had to keep such a big secret all these years. LeAnn just wants a normal life with a normal sister. Someone she could share her secrets with and gossip about her latest crush. Which so happened to be Cameron Haze. Taylor despised his father.

Taylor had to stop being her aunt and focus on just being her sister. All she wanted to do was protect her like a parent... like an aunt. She needed to be supportive and let LeAnn experience things first like an older sister should. She owed her that much.

LeAnn felt the pressure to lose her virginity like Taylor. She was older and wanted to experience everything first. Her older brother Chase got to experience everything first. So why shouldn't she?

Later that night she snuck out of the house to meet up with Cameron at his hotel. She was going to go all the way. When she walked into the hotel room she took off all her clothes. Cameron was surprised.

"Are you sure?" He asked. LeAnn nodded and took his hand and placed it upon her breast. He leaned in and kissed her as they made their way to the bed.

Chapter 9

LeAnn was grinning form ear to ear the morning she came home. She snuck into Taylor's bedroom and got underneath her covers. Taylor woke up to the sound of LeAnn's breathing. "What are you doing up so early? Did you just get in?" Taylor asked in her sleepy voice.

"Yes... Guess where I was." LeAnn giggled. "Where?" Taylor asked. She wasn't in the mood for her guessing games. "First, are you my little sister right now or my aunt?" LeAnn asked. "I'm your sister! What LeAnn? I'm trying to sleep!" Taylor said annoyingly. "Cameron and I had sex last night." LeAnn giggled as she put her hands up to her mouth with excitement.

Taylors eyes opened wide. She was wide awake now. "Why would she do this? We're not competing with each other! I've known Alex forever and she's known Cameron for five minutes!" Taylor thought to herself.

She was furious! "And of all the people, why the son of Joshua Haze?" Taylor wondered.

"Are you going to say anything?" LeAnn asked. She was upset that she hadn't acknowledged her yet. "I don't know what to say LeAnn." Taylor said.

"Well you don't sound happy for me." LeAnn said.

"I'm confused why you'd go out and have sex for the first time as soon as I told you I did." Taylor confessed.

"Well, I'm not jealous of you if that's where you're going with this." LeAnn said.

"No, but it sounds like you're competing with me." Taylor said.

"Competing with what exactly? You're an eighteen- year old girl who slept with someone who's old enough to be her dad!" LeAnn exclaimed.

"You know about that situation, so why would you say that?" Taylor asked. She felt hurt that LeAnn would say something like that. It wasn't fair for her to throw that in her face. "I should have never told her." She thought.

"I'm going to bed." LeAnn said as she stormed out of Taylors bedroom. Taylor knew she was holding on to a lot of anger for having to keep this secret. She had never seen this side of her before. She feared that LeAnn wouldn't keep this secret for long. This is the angriest she had ever seen her.

She didn't want this secret to ruin their relationship. She stressed out about it all day. The only other person she could talk to was Alex. She feared he would eventually resent her like LeAnn does. She didn't know what to do.

She was crying by the time she got to Alex's house. "What's wrong?" He asked. "Do you feel that knowing my secret is a burden?" She asked.

"No. I think it's a miracle. You're getting a second chance to live a full life." He said. It was easy for him to believe that. He knew her in the past. LeAnn only knows Taylor.

"I think this secret is hurting LeAnn. All she wants is a sister and I don't know how to be her sister." Taylor cried. "She's young. When she's older she'll realize how close this made you two... and as for being someone's sister, you were Blakes sister. Try to remember what that's like." Alex comforted.

"It only hurts her because she loves you." He continued. "I hope so." Taylor said. "I have something for you." Alex said as he went into the other room. When he came out of the room he had a jewelry box in his hand. "Do you remember this?" He asked as he opened the box.

Taylor smiled. "That's the necklace you gave me for my birthday... when I felt I had nothing to celebrate." She replied. "Do you remember what I told you?" He asked. Taylor nodded. "Life is like a changing season." She replied.

Alex smiled. It was all the more proof that she was in fact Jordan. "Exactly, and you're a new leaf. This life is a new beginning for you. There's no burden in that." Alex said as he put the necklace around her neck.

"He always had a way with words." She thought. This was one of the reasons she loved him so deeply. He had a heart made of gold. He always knew how to make her feel better. He knew her like no one else. He understood her and has always been such a good listener. She's never had these kinds of conversations with anyone. He knew her deeply. She knew there was no one else for her. He was her soulmate. They belonged together.

This is the kind of love she wanted LeAnn to have. She thought that Cameron could never give the kind of love she deserves, because of who his father was. There's that expression "Like father like son". She was sure that someone raised by someone like Joshua Haze, would grow up to be just like him.

The next day Taylor waited for LeAnn to come home. She wanted to apologize to her. She wanted to tell her that she was happy she found someone she cared about. Even though deep down she didn't agree with it.

Her friend jack stopped by. "So, Alison said you started seeing someone." He said.

"Alison has such a big mouth." Taylor thought. She didn't want a lot of people knowing. She couldn't let Blake and Brit to find out cause then they'd want to meet this mystery guy their daughter is spending all her time with. "So, who's the guy?" Jack asked.

"No one you know. My parents don't even know, so don't say anything." Taylor said.

"Why are you keeping it a secret from your parents?" Jack asked.

"Because then they'd want to invite him to dinner and embarrass me. I'm not ready for that. My parents can be so nosey." Taylor explained.

Jack laughed, but inside it was hurting him. He had always had the biggest crush on her. He never had the courage to tell her. He always thought that she was too good for him. She was rich and he wasn't. He didn't have a trust fund and an easy path to college. He had to work hard for everything.

"So, there's this gallery for local artists. The photo's I took of you were selected for a show case. It's next Friday. Will you come?" He asked.

"Of course, I'll go! I wouldn't miss it for the world. Congratulations!" Taylor exclaimed.

"Thank you, I'm really excited about it." Jack said.

Taylor was so happy for him. He knew exactly what he wanted and wasn't afraid to go after his dreams.

"So, are Alison and I going to get to meet this new guy?" He asked. She knew her friends would never understand, and she knew that they could never meet him. "I don't know... I don't even know how serious this is or if it would even work." She said. She didn't even know if her family would accept it. "This isn't fair! What kind of life is this if I can't be with the one I love and share my life with." She thought.

"Well there's no sense in stringing him along if you don't think it's going to work." Jack said.

"We're just having fun for now." Taylor said. "So, they're just using each other for sex? Lucky guy." Jack thought. He'd give anything just to have her once. He would indulge in her and make it last as long as possible. He desired her more than anyone else. He's never wanted anyone the way he wanted her. All he could hope for was that she'd cut this guy loose so he could make her his.

"Well, I have to get going. I have a lot to do before the big show case." Jack said. "Okay, I'll see you next Friday then." Taylor replied.

Later that day when LeAnn came home, Taylor was waiting for her in her bedroom. LeAnn walked in and set her purse on the dresser. "I'm sorry." Taylor said.

Leann turned around and saw Taylor sitting on her bed. She was still upset with her. All she wanted was to have a normal family with a normal sister. She wanted to experience things first and felt that she was robbed of that right.

"I am happy that you found someone that you really care about, and I hope he feels the same for you. Sometimes I just feel protective over you." Taylor explained.

"Sometimes I just feel that you're more protective like an aunt." LeAnn replied.

"I know. I promise I'll work on it. I'm closer to you than anyone else. Besides Alex, you're the only one who knows my secret." Taylor said.

"I guess it has given us a special kind of bond. I never thought of it like that. I've just always longed for a relationship with my sister." LeAnn cried.

"In a way you get both." Taylor said. LeAnn nodded. She never really thought of it that way. She always felt that it was a burden when really it was a blessing. She knew their father would swim across the ocean just to see Jordan one more time.

"So, do you forgive me?" Taylor asked. "Always, and I'm sorry for what I said, you know about you sleeping with a man old enough to be your dad. I didn't mean it. I was just angry." She said.

"I know. It's okay. After all, sisters tend to fight about dumb stuff." Taylor said. LeAnn smiled in between her tears and laughter. "They do don't they." She replied. "You're the sister I never had. I love you." Taylor said.

"I love you too. I hate fighting with you." LeAnn said.

"Me too. So, my friend Jack is having some of his photograph in an art gallery next Friday. What do you say about you and Cameron coming with me. I'm sure they'll be an after party we can go to." Taylor asked.

"You don't like parties." LeAnn said. "True, but my sister does." Taylor replied. LeAnn was so happy that they made up and that she invited her and Cameron to the art gallery. This made her feel like they really were sisters. This was the kind of things sisters would do… just hang out without that awkward feeling of her being her aunt. It meant the world to her that she invited Cameron to go.

"Are you going to invite Alex?" LeAnn asked. "I can't. I don't want anyone to find out about us yet. I don't know how I'm going to get anyone to accept that we love each other." Taylor said.

"I'm sorry you have to keep this a secret. I was actually thinking of having Cameron meet the parents." LeAnn said. Taylor felt her heart drop into her stomach. She knew Blake would never approve. Blake knew all about Jordan's history with Joshua Haze. There was no way he would allow his daughter to date his son. She knew Leann was in for a major heartbreak.

She wanted to warn her, but they just made up. "Should I tell her and risk her being angry at me again? Or watch her get her heart broken because her dad forbids it?" Taylor wondered.

Chapter 10

Taylor was working the front desk at the hotel when Jack came running in with excitement. His photos made the newspaper along with a few other local artists.

It read;

"Local artists showcase their art work at Galley's Art Gallery this Friday at 6:00 pm. Bid on your favorite art pieces. Money goes towards their college education. Join us in supporting these local talents!"

"This is amazing!" Taylor exclaimed.

"I can't believe they selected one of my photos to be in the newspaper. This is huge!" Jack said.

He hoped that having his photos selected for the art gallery would help him get into a good college. The fact that it made it into the newspaper was just the icing on the cake!

"This is going to look so good on your college applications." Taylor said.

"This is the biggest thing I've ever had happen to me. I feel like this is my calling. I was born to do this." Jack said.

Taylor was so happy for him. She felt blessed that she could share this experience with him. She supported both of her friends in their dreams. She couldn't wait to see it all come together on his big day.

"I invited LeAnn and Cameron. I'll tell them to invite their friends too." Taylor said.

"Thank you! That would be awesome." Jack replied.

That evening while Taylor was at Alex's house she found herself thinking about the future. She sat out on the four-season porch wrapped in a blanket while sipping hot tea.

"What's going on in that beautiful head of yours?" Alex asked. He could always tell when she was deep in thought. She has always had that same look on her face, even when she was Jordan. Lost in a gaze.

"Everyone around me seems to know what they're doing with their life except me. LeAnn is able to bring her boyfriend out in public and no one looks their way gawking. Jack and Alison know what career they want to do and I feel more confused than I have ever been. I don't know what I want to do with my life. I don't even know how I'm going to get everyone to accept us as a couple. I hate having all these secrets." Taylor confessed.

"Everything will work itself out. Some things may just take a little more time, but the beauty in you getting a second chance is that you have a lifetime to figure it out. Most people don't know what they want to do. So, they try many things until they find that one thing that sets their soul on fire." Alex encouraged.

He always made great points. What she feared the most was living a life without him in it. What if Blake and Brit don't understand or believe her when she tells them that she's really Jordan? What if her grandparents don't believe her either? She couldn't live without her family and she would hate to have to choose between them and Alex.

What she questioned the most was, if she's meant to live a new life as Taylor or hold onto who she used to be in her past life. She desperately wanted to be with Alex. But her family only knows her as Taylor... Their daughter.... Grand-daughter. They'd never believe she was really Jordan, not when they've had eighteen years believing she's Taylor.

She had this constant feeling of doubt. If she couldn't convince everyone who she really was, then what would her future look like for her and Alex? She didn't want to choose between them, and honestly, she knew that Alex wouldn't let her. He would end up choosing for her. He would let her go because he would never take her away from her family. He would want her to live her life to the fullest with no regrets.

She wondered if he had given that any thought. They can't keep their relationship a secret forever. She knew he was holding onto hope that her family would believe her and accept them as a couple... But she feared the cold reality that they wouldn't.

She hated that they couldn't be seen in public together for the fear of someone seeing them. They couldn't go to a movie or out to dinner like normal couples. It felt like a dirty little secret. She even had to go to the art gallery dateless while LeAnn gets to bring her date. It just wasn't fair. If she's not able to be with Alex, then what is the purpose of her being alive again?

They couldn't just keep sneaking around and hiding in his house like hermits. Having to park her car a mile down the road in a hidden spot where he'd pick her up. If people were to find out they would only see it as a grown man taking advantage of a teenage girl and using her for sex. It made her wonder if they were ever going to have a future together. People would always look at them in disgust or think she's his daughter. Does he think about that kind of future? Does he fear what Blake would do to him if he found out? All these questions ran over and over in her head on repeat.

"This is never going to work." She thought while Alex flipped through the newspaper. "Your friends photos are in the paper. Are you going to the art gallery this Friday?" He asked.

"Yeah. I invited LeAnn and Cameron. I would have invited you, but no one knows about us yet." Taylor explained.

"I understand. That's probably best." He replied.

"What's that supposed to mean?" Taylor thought. "Does he even want anyone to know about us? How long does he want to keep us a secret?" She wondered.

"I have to go." She snapped.

"What's wrong?" He asked. "Nothing. I just have to leave." She replied with an attitude.

"Don't say nothing. I've known you for a long time and I can tell when you're upset." Alex said.

"If you don't want anyone to know about us then tell me now so I can save myself the heartache!" She yelled.

She always had a little temper when she was upset, which he had always thought was adorable. It brought back memories when she was Jordan and she threw a protein shake at him. Luckily there wasn't anything in reach for her to throw.

"I never said I didn't want anyone to know. I would love to shout from the roof top that I'm in love with you! But, this is a complicated situation. I want it to be the right timing when we tell everyone. I want your family to believe you when you tell them who you are and let it sink in before telling them about us." Alex explained.

He knew if they told everyone who she was and that they were dating, it would be too much news at once. Which could result in a huge blow out fight.

Taylor burst into tears. "I just hate that we can't go out and do anything together. I hate that we have to hide this." She cried.

Alex took her in his arms. "It won't be forever, I promise. We'll just take it one day at a time. One step at a time. Trust me." Alex said.

He was terrified to tell Blake that he was dating Taylor before he knew who she really was. He knew it would ruin their friendship. He feared that Blake wouldn't accept them together even if he believed she was really Jordan because the last eighteen years he's only known her to be his daughter. There's already a bond formed to protect her. He loved her and was willing to risk everything, but just wanted it to be the right timing.

He hated to see her hurting like this. He would do anything for her even if Blake killed him. "I'll tell them when golf season is over. I'll let some time pass, so it can sink in before telling him about us." Taylor said.

That Friday the gallery was packed full of people. Taylor could tell how nervous Jack was. She noticed that he kept wiping the sweat off his hands onto the side of his pants before shaking hands with people who came to admire his work. He was trying so hard for people not to notice, but Taylor noticed.

"You're very talented!" One lady said as she gazed at his photographs. "Thank you!" Jack replied. "A beautiful model too!" One mans voice said. Taylor knew that voice. She looked through the crowd to see who it was. Joshua Haze. He was practically drooling over the photographs.

"He's such a pig." Taylor thought. She found a way to squeeze through the crowd to keep a distance. She didn't want to be anywhere near Joshua. "What is he even doing here? He hates art." She wondered. Then she thought that maybe Cameron invited him. She hated that LeAnn was dating Joshua's son. She remembered that the only reason he was so eager to marry Jordan was to get in on her family's wealth. On top of that he slept with numerous women while he was engaged to her. She wondered if he was getting Cameron to pursue LeAnn for the same reason.

"Are you okay?" LeAnn asked. "Yeah. It was getting too crowded over there." Taylor replied. "I'm sorry you couldn't bring Alex with you." LeAnn apologized. "It's fine. We'll be able to go out in public together eventually." Taylor replied.

LeAnn pointed over to Joshua Haze. "That's Cameron's dad. He invited him so that I could meet him. Things are getting serious between us. I think he's the one." LeAnn said.

"I'm happy for you." Taylor lied. She despised that they were together. She knew that family was only after one thing. "I am definitely bringing Cameron home to meet the parents." LeAnn stated.

Taylor felt her stomach turn into knots. She knew this was a bad idea. Blake will never approve.

Chapter 11

Taylor spent the next day at her grand-parent's house. It brought back so many memories of the life she once lived. They left Jordan's bedroom exactly, the same. It was as if they had never gotten over her death.

She sat in the living room flipping through old photo albums. The old photo's brought tears to her eyes. She missed her old life. Maybe if she had survived, she and Alex would still be together and have a family of their own. She wasn't sure how to live in this new life or who she was supposed to be. She didn't know where she fit in.

"Jordan was such a free spirit." Her Grandma said from the hallway. "How do you mean?" Taylor asked. She never felt that way. She felt she had always tried to live up to everyone's expectations instead of her own. Like helping with the family business and getting engaged to a pro golfer.

"She wasn't always. She went through a lot when she got sick, but she had this light inside her that I always knew was there. Once she made up her mind about something there was no telling her no. That light inside her started to shine through, I don't think she ever saw that though. Maybe if she'd been given a longer life she would have come to see it in herself." Susan said.

"Do you still miss her?" Taylor asked.

"Every single day." Susan replied as she walked over next to her to gaze at the photos. "You remind me of her. You look so much like her and you have her personality." Susan said. "How so?" Taylor asked. "You have a light about you too. You care so much about everyone's wellbeing. You're also a bit stubborn like she was, but you have a heart of gold. You're sensitive and sentimental." Susan explained.

Taylor wanted to tell her that the reason she reminded her so much of Jordan is because she is Jordan. She wanted to tell her that she didn't have to miss her anymore because she was here... But, she didn't want to ruin a perfect moment.

It could go one of two ways. She would either believe her and cry and hug, making the moment more perfect than what it already was... Or, she wouldn't believe her and think it was some cruel joke and ruin the moment. So, she chose not to say a word.

She was beginning to think that maybe she needed to let go of her old life and live in this new life that she'd been given. Even if that meant breaking things off with Alex.

This secret would crush her and the whole family. It could ruin them and things would never be the same.

She needed to experience new things. She needed to do things an eighteen-year old girl would do. Go to college, party, and make bad decisions. In her old life she always focused on pleasing everyone else. She thought material things were everything so she surrounded herself with wealthy people. Now all she wanted was to experience life from a new perspective.

She wanted to see the world, party at some random bar in New York, watch someone play guitar in hopes a random stranger will throw some quarters in their guitar case. She wanted to do things that she never got to experience in her past life. The only problem is that none of these things include Alex, because her family would never approve of their relationship. It would break her heart to leave Alex. He's the love of her life.

The more she thought about it, the more she realized that she could never leave him. Her heart felt torn. She desperately wanted her family to know who she really was, but she knew that no one would believe her. So, for now she had to keep these secrets to herself. It weighed so heavily on her heart.

A couple of days past and Taylor was working an evening shift at the hotel counter. Her nerves were revved up. She kept looking at the clock, knowing that LeAnn and Cameron were out to dinner with their parents. She knew the evening was not going to end well. Blake will not approve of Cameron dating his daughter. Especially when he finds out he's the son of Joshua Haze.

Taylor did a lot of pacing back and forth, biting her nails, and continuously glancing at the clock. "Are you nervous about something?" Jack asked, who was working the counter with her. "No, why would you ask that?" Taylor asked nervously. "Because you haven't been able to stand still since you got here and you keep biting your nails." Jack replied.

"He knows me so well." Taylor thought to herself. "My sister brought her new boyfriend to meet our parents. I'm just hoping it all goes well." Taylor confessed. "Well why wouldn't it? Cameron seems like a nice guy and his dad is a famous pro golfer." Jack said.

"You're right. I don't know why I'm worried." Taylor laughed as if she was just being ridiculous when in reality she was trying to hide the fact that she was still nervous.

"His dad payed a pretty penny for those pictures of you. He's such a nice guy. Thanks to him I'll have money to help pay for college." Jack said.

She tried to act happy for him, but the fact that Joshua had pictures of her just flat out disgusted her. "He's such a pig." She thought. She knew Joshua didn't buy those pictures to simply help a struggling high school kid go to college. Joshua hated her family because of the messy break up with Jordan. All he ever wanted was to get his grubby hands on their family business. As soon as he found out Jordan was dying he tried to rush marriage so he could inherit what Jordan had. She was sure he was only out for revenge.

Not only that, but he was also a cheating bastard. He didn't know what love was. Let alone an act of kindness. "You're worrying again. Is there something else going on?" jack asked. "Of course not! I'm stopping. No more worrying." Taylor said as she pulled her finger tips away from her mouth.

Just then LeAnn stormed into the hotel. "We need to talk!" LeAnn snapped. "Okay… Are you okay here for a few minutes?" Taylor asked Jack. "Yeah of course." Jack said. He was a little suspicious as to why LeAnn would be so angry at Taylor. Jack thought Taylor was perfect. He knew she would never do anything to intentionally hurt anyone.

Taylor and LeAnn walked outside back by the dumpsters. "Are you okay?" Taylor asked nervously. She knew what this was about. She knew Blake didn't approve of Cameron because of who his father is. She felt responsible. Nothing like having your past come around and bite you in the ass. She knew she should have warned her, but at the same time she knew that Cameron and his family was no good for her. She even wondered if Joshua plotted having Cameron date LeAnn in order to get his hands on the family business.

"Why didn't you tell me that you use to be engaged to Cameron's dad?" LeAnn demanded. "I should have told you, but that was a long time ago." Taylor confessed. "Damn right you should have told me! I just made a fool out of myself! My dad wouldn't even give him a chance when I introduced him at dinner! He forbids us to see one another and when I questioned why, he told me all about Joshua and his precious sister Jordan! You ruined my life!" LeAnn cried.

"I'm so sorry. I understand how upsetting this is, but honestly that family would have ruined you. His dad wants nothing more than to get his filthy hands on our family business." Taylor explained.

"Really? And what do you think he'd do if he found out you're fucking his best friend? Fucking Jordan's man?" LeAnn yelled.

"That's different. One, Alex would never ruin us, and two, I am Jordan! I never snitched on you!" Taylor yelled. "It's not different! He would forbid you to see him! In fact, he would think that's worse than me and Cameron dating! He would feel betrayed! I have kept all your secrets and you hide the biggest secret of all from me! A secret that you knew would crush me! How many more people are you going to lie to?" LeAnn screamed.

"I'm really sorry. Look, maybe I can talk to Blake. Maybe I can convince him to give Cameron a chance. We'll figure this out." Taylor begged. She didn't want Blake to find out about her and Alex. Not until she proved to him who she really was.

"I don't want your help! You've done enough! I just want you to stay the hell out of my life!" LeAnn yelled and stormed off.

She had never seen LeAnn this hurt before in all her life. She knew it'd take more than an apology to earn her forgiveness. She knew she messed up big time. She trusted her with so many secrets, but she was afraid to tell her this one. She gasped for a breath as tears rolled down her face.

She worried that LeAnn wouldn't keep her secret anymore, and honestly, she didn't blame her. She knew she had to warn Alex. She stood there for a moment and tried to calm herself down. She couldn't go home to where LeAnn was. She needed to give her some space. She texted Blake and told him she was staying the night at Alison's house. Then texted Alex telling him she was coming over.

She had to warn him. She knew that they'd have to stop seeing each other for a while.

She could feel her heart breaking when she arrived at his house. "How did life get to be so complicated?" She wondered. Her last life wasn't perfect. It's taken her a second life to figure out exactly what she wanted, but it came with huge mountains to climb, betrayal and secrets.

She walked inside and felt her heart shatter into a million pieces. Alex had thrown together a romantic candle lit dinner. He was thinking they'd have a romantic night together and she came here to break up with him.

"Are you hungry beautiful?" He asked. Taylors eyes immediately filled with tears and she began to sob. "You're the perfect man. This isn't fair." She cried. Alex took her in his arms and wiped the tears off her cheeks. "What's wrong?" He asked.

"LeAnn found out about Joshua Haze. Blake forbid her to see Cameron Haze. She's furious with me and I don't know if she'll keep our secret anymore. I'm afraid she's going to tell Blake about us." She explained.

"Then let her. I love you. I'm not going to lose you again. There's nothing that's going to stop me from spending the rest of my life with you." Alex said.

"It's not that simple Alex. In this life we're not the same age. In Blakes eyes, I'm his daughter in this life. He would be furious and he'll never believe that I'm Jordan! He'd never allow us to be together!" Taylor yelled.

"Tell him who you are and try to convince him." Alex said. "He'd never believe it. Maybe we're just not meant to be together like we hoped." Taylor said.

"I don't believe that. You came back for a reason. I'm not going to lose you again." Alex argued. "I'm afraid we don't have a choice." Taylor said. They both became silent. This was killing them inside. "Life's way of playing a cruel joke." Alex thought.

"I should go." Taylor said quietly as she fought back more tears. As she turned to walk away he took her by the hand and pulled her into his arms and kissed her. She pulled off his shirt and he picked her up as she wrapped her legs around his waist. He carried her into the bedroom and gently put her down on the bed. "I don't want to let you go... at least not tonight." He whispered in her ear.

Chapter 12

LeAnn thought it was about time she had some secrets of her own. She wasn't going to let Jordan's past affect her life. She has always been a good girl. She was a good daughter who had always done what she was suppose to. She was a good sister, a good niece who kept Taylors secrets.

She and Cameron began sneaking around to see each other. Even if it was only for an hour. They would drive to a hidden spot in the woods to make love. "Maybe we should just get married." LeAnn suggested to Cameron. "You know your dad wouldn't approve of that." Cameron stated. "I don't care. Maybe that's the only way he'd accept that we're together." She said.

"I think that would make it worse. I love you LeAnn, and I know you'd want your family at our wedding. You'd want their love and support. I don't want you to do something you'd regret later." Cameron explained. "The only thing I'll regret is not being with you." LeAnn said.

"I want your family to like me, and I don't think they ever would if we did that. I'd always be the guy who stole their daughter. I want to have their permission." Cameron said. "I understand where you're coming from, but we're going behind their back now." LeAnn pointed out.

"That's different. Your father would think of me as a thief if I married you and whisked you away. I want our wedding and marriage to be perfect. I want to plan my proposal to you. As romantic as it'd be to run off and elope, I know deep down you'd want a traditional wedding, where your father could give you away, I just need to earn his approval." Cameron said.

"How are you going to win his approval? He hates your father." LeAnn asked. "I don't know yet, but I'll think of something. Somehow, I'll prove to him that I'm nothing like my dad and that my intentions are pure. I'll do whatever it takes. I'm not giving up." Cameron said.

"Pure intentions huh? Meeting out here to have sex in your car isn't so pure." LeAnn joked as she climbed over to the driver's side in her short yellow sundress. "Well, maybe not this part." He whispered as he pulled down the straps to her dress. He pulled her body closer so his mouth could reach her breasts. He ran his hand up her thigh and up her dress. "No panties? If I had to guess, I'd say you came here with naughty intentions." He whispered. "Guess my intentions aren't as pure as yours." She said as she leaned in and kissed him.

He was so in love with her. He knew that he wanted to spend the rest of his life with her. He knew that he was nothing like his father, but how could he prove that to her family?

He often wondered why his mother stayed with his father. She knew all about his cheating. They've had many arguments about it. Was it because she signed a prenuptial agreement and knew she wouldn't be able to live the lifestyle she does now? That was the only reason he could think of.

His mother was one of his one-night stands, but unlike the others, she ended up pregnant. Joshua was so protective of his public image that he married her and acted as if the pregnancy was planned to please the public eye.

His mother had no college degree and no rich family. Just a rich cheating husband. They tried to keep it a secret from Cameron about how they met, but he had heard many of their arguments and knew the truth. Joshua had told Cameron's mother that she'd have nothing if it weren't for him. He made all the money so he could sleep with whoever he wanted to and that he only married her because she was pregnant.

He despised his father for how he treated his mother, but at the same time he loved him too. After all, he was his father. He knew that he didn't want to be anything like his dad. He wanted love and a happy marriage. The only thing he admired about his dad was his successful golf career.

Cameron wanted to take care of LeAnn, love her and be faithful to her. All he had to do was figure out how to prove to her family that his intentions are to be loyal to her and to love her the way she deserved.

Later that day LeAnn came home and saw that Taylor was home. "Where have you been?" Taylor asked. "I don't see how that's any of your business. You're my younger sister, not my parent." LeAnn responded. "I was just curious." Taylor responded. "I was out with friends." LeAnn snapped.

"How are your friends? Anything new with them?" Taylor asked hoping to start up a friendly conversation. She wanted to work things out. She didn't want LeAnn to stay mad at her. "Nope! Same old stuff." LeAnn responded.

"Alex and I broke up." Taylor blurted out in hopes that telling something so personal would help mend their broken fences. "Maybe that's for the best." LeAnn responded as she sat on the end of her bed to take her shoes off.

"You can't stay mad at me forever. You're the person I tell everything to." Taylor pleaded. "Wow, not everything." LeAnn snapped as she stood up and walked to her bedroom door to show Taylor the way out.

"LeAnn please." Taylor begged. "Get out of my room!" LeAnn yelled. Taylor walked out of her bedroom, but as soon as she turned around to say one more thing LeAnn slammed the door in her face. She knew LeAnn wasn't planning to forgive her anytime soon. All she could do was give her some space.

Throughout the weeks LeAnn continued to sneak around with Cameron. A part of her found it exciting to be a little rebellious. Another part of her was sad inside. She had always strived to make her parents proud of her. Her parents' opinion was so important to her. One of her biggest fears was disappointing them. She wanted so desperately for them to like Cameron and approve of their relationship. She feared that if they found out they'd been sneaking around that they'd never approve.

Cameron had tried talking to her dad, but with no luck. Her dad continued to give him the cold shoulder. This hurt LeAnn more than words could ever explain. "Why can't he just give him the benefit of the doubt for me? Why can't he trust my decisions?" She wondered.

She was twenty years old. She shouldn't have to fight this hard for her dads' permission. He left her with no choice but to sneak around.

While Cameron was busy with practice today, she got herself dolled up to see him later that night. She curled her long blonde hair, wore his favorite sweet, smelling perfume, and wore a short white sundress with cute buttons in the front. "Easy access. Only four more hours until I see him." She thought.

Just then her phone rang with an unfamiliar number. "Hello?" She answered. "Hey this is Joshua! Cameron's dad."

"Oh hi Mr. Haze!" She responded. "I was wondering if you could meet me for lunch today. Cameron is busy, and I have some really important news." He explained. "Yeah of course! I'm not seeing him until tonight." She replied. "Perfect! Can you head over now?" He asked. "Yes, I'll see you soon." She replied.

"At least his dad approves of us dating." She thought. She didn't understand why Blake thought he was so bad. "Yes, he cheated on Jordan, but that was over twenty years ago. People change." She thought.

When she got to his house he greeted her with a smile. "Come on in! I ordered us take out." He said. "I love take out." She replied. He guided her out back to have lunch on the patio. He then poured her a glass of wine. "Oh, I'm not old enough just yet." She said. "It can be our little secret." He said. She smiled and took a sip of the wine.

She loved that he was treating her like an adult. Her father still treats her like she's sixteen. Joshua sat across from her smiling and admiring her little white sundress. He always admired the younger women.

"You don't mind keeping secrets, do you?" He asked. "What do you mean?" She asked. "Well, Cameron told me that you two have been seeing each other in secret because your father doesn't approve." Joshua explained.

"Oh that. We're trying to figure out how Cameron can win my fathers approval. He's very picky on who I date. You know dads can be over protective." She said.

"Well, why don't you tell your dad that you're a grown twenty-year old woman and that you can make your own choices." He suggested.

"It's not that simple." She replied. "You're afraid of disappointing your dad. That's a tough one. Parents never look at their children the same once they disappoint them." Joshua said.

"Yeah, that's what I'm afraid of." LeAnn said sadly. "Have you thought of what you'd do if your dad found out?" Joshua asked. "I don't know. I'm hoping that he doesn't. It would ruin everything." She replied.

Joshua grabbed a vanilla envelope from the chair next to him, stood up and walked behind LeAnn and set it in front of her. "What is this?" She asked. "Open it." He said.

She opened it and pulled out numerous photos of her and Cameron having sex in his car. Naked, raw, and closeup photos. Tears began to roll down her face. "What do you want?" She asked. He pulled her long blond hair away from her neck and whispered in her ear. "I think you know what I want. Text Cameron and cancel your plans for the day." Then he slowly kissed her neck.

She felt disgusted and uncomfortable. "I can't." She cried. "Okay, then I'll just send these photos to your dad. It's the right thing to do." He said as he snatched the photos from her hand. "No wait!" She cried.

"Text Cameron and cancel your plans." He demanded. Her hands were shaking as she did what she was told. Her legs were shaking. Her heart was pounding. "Here's the deal. I have ten photos. Each time you fuck me, you earn one back. Then this mess will be all over." He said.

LeAnn began to sob. "Stop crying! No one wants to fuck a cry baby! Aren't you a woman?" He shouted. She did what she was told and stopped crying. She was terrified. She wiped the tears off her face and took a deep breath. Pushing her fears deep down in the pit of her stomach.

Joshua grabbed the back of her hair and kissed her lips. He unbuttoned her sundress and unfastened her bra to expose her breasts. He ran his hands up her dress. "I love a girl that wears no panties to lunch." He whispered.

Chapter 13

When LeAnn got home she locked herself in her bedroom. She let out a scream in anger and pain followed be tears. She ripped up the photo of her and Cameron having sex. Her mother, Brit knocked on the door. "Are you okay?" She yelled through the door. "I'm fine mom! I just stubbed my toe!" LeAnn yelled back as she tried to silence her crying.

She took off her white sundress and threw it in the trash next to her desk. She got in the shower and scrubbed her body until it was beat red. No matter how hard she scrubbed she could still feel his hands, mouth, and body on hers.

After her long shower she put on a pair of sweatpants and sweatshirt and buried herself underneath her blankets. She felt dirty, disgusting, humiliated, ashamed, and angry. She stayed in bed all evening and woke up to her phone ringing. It was Cameron. She immediately clicked it to voicemail.

She couldn't bare to face him. Not after what happened today. This was something she could never tell him, and he wouldn't understand why she suddenly lost the desire for him to touch her in any way. She didn't want anyone to touch her. Especially Joshua Haze, but she knew she had no other choice if she wanted to get the other nine pictures. The thought of having to have sex with him nine more times sickened her.

There was another knock at her bedroom door. "LeAnn are you okay?" Taylor asked. "Go away! The door is locked for a reason!" LeAnn yelled.

Taylor sensed something was wrong. It wasn't like her to hide in her room all day. "Did she and Cameron break up?" She wondered.

LeAnn's phone kept ringing. Cameron was calling her every fifteen minutes. After sending him to voicemail three times he finally texted her. "It's not like you to not answer your phone. Hope everything is okay." He texted. She felt bad and didn't want to leave him hanging. "I'm really sick. I'm going to bed." She texted back.

She hated that she had to lie to him. She hated what his father was making her do. "So much for a happily ever after." She thought.

"I wish I could see you. I'd make you chicken noodle soup." Cameron texted. She couldn't respond back. She squeezed her cell phone tight and began to sob. There was no longer a future for them. She knew she had to break up with him, so she'd never end up in this situation again.

She blamed Taylor. If her past self never dated Joshua, she would not be in this mess. She would have been allowed to date Cameron and wouldn't have been blackmailed into having sex with his dad. She hated Taylor... She hated Jordan! Because of her, her life was ruined.

She blamed her dad. If Blake wouldn't have held a grudge against Joshua, she could have dated Cameron. But her fear of disappointing him and being humiliated put her in this situation. She hated him. She hated all of them. She hated herself. She hated herself for not being brave, for not being strong, and for not telling Joshua no.

She should have stood up for herself, she should have stood up to her father regardless of how disappointed he'd be. She made up her mind right then and there that she was not going to let Blake, Taylor, or Joshua control her. She was so angry and disgusted at this point that she didn't care if Joshua sent those pictures to Blake.

She was done. Even if Blake wanted to cut her out of the family business. She didn't care. She didn't want anyone to hurt her ever again.

It didn't take long for Joshua to get a hold of her again. Within a couple of days, he texted her, "Come now. Wear something slutty."

Fear took over her body. Her heart began to race in fear. Her palms began to sweat, and her hands began to shake. Her eyes filled with tears. She couldn't go through this again. She suddenly didn't feel brave anymore.

With her shaking hands she texted back, "I have to work." He replied, "Call in, or I'm sending these pictures to your dad."

She was afraid to tell him no. He had the power to completely ruin her life. The fear was so intense that it clouded her mind and she couldn't think clearly. So, she did as she was told. She put on a short black dress and knee-high boots and went to his house.

The sound of his heavy breathing while on top of her made her physically ill. She felt disgusting. She held back the tears and shut every emotion off. She became numb to his pain. As if she was just a dead piece of flesh he was inserting himself into. He had taken her body from her. He took away her right to choose. She refused to let him see her pain. She didn't want him to know that he broke her heart too.

When she got home she vigorously scrubbed her body in the shower. She couldn't take the sick feeling anymore and began throwing up in the shower. The numb feeling that masked her emotions wore off. Her body physically felt heavy with all the emotion she was carrying.

She sat down in the shower and watch the vomit wash down the drain. "I can't keep doing this." She cried.

When she got out of the shower she crawled underneath the blankets on her bed. She looked at her phone and saw she had three missed calls and a text from Cameron. "I don't know what's going on. Are you still sick? I haven't heard from you in days." The text read.

She didn't respond. She just set her phone on the end table next to her bed. She literally didn't know what to say to him. She couldn't tell anyone what was going on, especially Cameron.

She couldn't bare the thought of looking at him and lying. She couldn't bare the thought of breaking his heart by dumping him. "Maybe if I just avoid him, he'll give up on me." She thought.

She grabbed her phone once more and blocked his number, so he could no longer text or call her. She didn't want to give in. It broke her every time she saw a text from him. She felt bad for ignoring him. Blocking him was a sure way to not feel that pain anymore. "Out of sight, out of mind." She thought.

She didn't want to lie, but she didn't want to tell the truth either. She felt ashamed, embarrassed, and like she did something wrong. "Goodbye Cameron." She whispered before falling asleep.

Chapter 14

Cameron was worried about LeAnn. He knew he couldn't talk to her dad since her dad despised his family. That only left her younger sister Taylor. One night while Taylor was at work, he went down to the hotel lobby.

"Can I talk to you for a minute?" He asked. Taylor wanted to tell him no, but she wanted LeAnn's forgiveness even more. So, she agreed to talk to him. "Meet me by the dumpsters out back in five minutes." She replied.

When she walked out there she saw him pacing back and forth. He looked nervous and upset. "What do you want to talk about?" She asked. "First of all, you have to promise me that whatever we talk about stays between us." He requested. "I promise." Taylor agreed.

He then explained what had been going on between him and LeAnn. How they have been seeing each other in secret. He explained how he tried to get Blake to give him a chance to prove that he's good for LeAnn. He expressed his love for her and the sudden silent treatment she had been giving him.

"I haven't talked to her in over a week. If I did something to upset her, I want to know. It's not like her to give me the silent treatment. Last I knew things were fine between us then all of sudden I don't hear from her anymore." He expressed.

Taylor knew all about her silent treatments. She wanted to tell him to get use to it and that's how LeAnn is, but she could see how upset and concerned he was. She didn't want to make it worse.

"I wish I could help you, but we're not on speaking terms right now." Taylor said. "Doesn't that worry you? You two are very close. It's not like her to give us the silent treatment." He said.

She could explain to him that LeAnn is really angry at Taylors past self for being engaged to his father, but then it would open up a conversation for a very long story that she didn't have the energy to make him believe.

"I'll try to talk to her. LeAnn has always been sensitive. She's probably just trying to work through some of her feelings." She explained.

"Well, here's my phone number. Can you text me to let me know if she's okay?" He asked as he handed her a piece of paper with his phone number on it. "Yeah, I will." She replied. "Thank you! I better go so I don't get you in trouble for talking to me... and I'm sorry for what my dad did to your Aunt Jordan. He hasn't been the greatest father or husband to my mom." He explained.

"It's okay. It's not like I ever knew my Aunt Jordan." She replied. At that moment she sensed that Cameron was nothing like Joshua. She had never known Joshua to be apologetic for anything, especially if it had nothing to do with him. Cameron is not the one who hurt her. It's not his fault he was raised by an awful man, and it seems that he has scars of his own from his father. He shouldn't have to pay the price for who his father is. "I have to fix this." Taylor thought.

She didn't hesitate to find out what was going on with LeAnn. As soon as she got home, she went straight to LeAnn's room to talk to her.

"I talked to Cameron tonight. He's worried about you." Taylor said. She stood in the doorway trying to respect her boundaries. LeAnn looked like a mess. She still had on baggy sweat pants and a sweatshirt from yesterday. Her hair wasn't even combed. It was just thrown up in a messy bun. "It's not like her to go days without dressing up and making herself look cute." Taylor thought.

"Well, it's over between us. The sooner he takes the hint the better." She replied. "Did he do something to hurt you?" Taylor asked. "No, I'm just not interested anymore! Now, leave me alone!" LeAnn yelled.

Taylor had this strong feeling that there was more to the story. She seemed angry, hurt, and depressed. Which made Taylor believe that she still loved him. "Love doesn't just fade away. It stays with you for eternity. Don't do something you'll regret later." Taylor said.

"I said leave!" LeAnn snapped as she stood up and pushed Taylor out of the doorway and slammed the door shut. "It's too late for that. I've already done something I regret." LeAnn thought to herself. She felt trapped. She didn't know how to get out of the mess that she was in and she felt like no one could help her.

Taylor was confused. "If Cameron didn't do anything wrong then why LeAnn's sudden change of heart? Unless, he did do something wrong and LeAnn doesn't want to tell me." Taylor thought.

She was determined to get to the bottom of it. She was going to find out exactly what happened. Even if she had to start snooping around. She texted Cameron and told him that LeAnn wouldn't tell her anything. After she texted him, she got a text from Alex.

"I miss you. I can't handle not seeing you. I love you so much. I don't care if your dad finds out. All I know is that I want to be with you for the rest of my life." Alex texted. Taylor missed him like crazy.

She began to think that maybe enough time has passed. No one would suspect anything. As far as LeAnn knew they had stopped seeing each other. LeAnn seemed to have enough of her own problems going on. She probably wouldn't even notice if Taylor started sneaking around with Alex again. So, she responded back to him. "I'll come over tonight. I love you too."

Another couple of days had passed and Joshua texted LeAnn again. "Ugh!" She groaned. She was so sick of this. She felt like she couldn't get away from him. She threw her phone on the bed in frustration. She felt like his puppet! He texts' and she had to come running. She hated that he had this control over her. Once again, she did as she was told.

When she got to his house he told her to take her clothes off in the living room. Joshua sat on the couch and watched her. "Come here." He ordered. He made her straddle him on the couch and began kissing her all over her body.

"What the HELL!!!"

LeAnn jumped up off Joshua and saw Cameron standing in entry way to the living room. She quickly picked up her dress to cover up her naked body. "Is this why you're not talking to me anymore!" Cameron screamed. "I can explain." LeAnn cried.

"I think what I just walked in on explains enough! You give me the silent treatment because you're fucking my father behind my back!" He yelled. His face was beet red and tears were flooding his eyes.

"Son, she came on to me. I tried to tell her no, but she wasn't taking no for an answer. You know how it is, you're a man. When a beautiful woman strips down naked in front of you... what was I supposed to do?" Joshua lied.

"You are such a liar!" LeAnn screamed. She quickly put on her sun dress and ran after Cameron as he was leaving.

"Cameron please, wait!" She cried. "I'm done with you both!" Cameron yelled. "Just let me explain myself, please!" She exclaimed.

Cameron turned around, "I was worried about you and wondering what I did wrong. And regardless of your father, I drove to your house to check on you, but saw you were leaving. So, I followed you. And here you are at my dad's house fucking his brains out! So, no! I don't want to hear your explanation! We're done!" He yelled and then got in his car and drove away.

LeAnn stood in the driveway sobbing. Joshua came out and stood next to her. "Well, looks like we'll have to rent a room from now on." He said.

Anger and rage filled her heart. She hated how cocky he was. He didn't even care that his own son was furious with him and may never forgive him. Joshua ruined her relationship with Cameron. At this point she didn't care if her father hated her too. This was their fault. She suddenly felt brave enough to stand up for herself. She just lost the love of her life!

"I don't think so! You ruined everything! Go ahead and send those pictures to my dad! I don't give a shit anymore!" She screamed.

Joshua slapped her across the face. "You think your dad is the only one I'd send those pictures to! I have news for you, I will spread them across the internet for the whole world to see! And if you think you're getting out of our deal, you're sadly mistaken. I know where you work and where you live. I'll find you where ever you go and take what I want! What you owe me!" He yelled as he grabbled her by the shoulders shaking her.

Fear paralyzed her entire body. She couldn't move. Everything in her was telling her to kick him and run, but she couldn't move. She was frozen in fear. He then grabbed her and threw her over his shoulders and took her inside to take what he wanted.

Chapter 15

LeAnn had never been so terrified in all her life. She was afraid to leave the house, afraid to go to work, afraid she's run into Cameron, or worse, run into Joshua. She wanted to tell Cameron the truth about what happened, but she felt guilty, embarrassed, ashamed, and angry.

She wanted Joshua dead. She wanted him to suffer the way that she is silently suffering. His text messages were getting more intense. She had been ignoring him, but he is now becoming more and more threatening. "I will find you when you least expect it. You can't ignore me forever." Was one text. "Eyes are watching your every move. I can't wait to get you alone. You'll wish you didn't ignore me." Was another text. He wouldn't stop. She knew she had to get out of here and out of this town.

She was so afraid that she stopped showing up for work. Taylor was concerned for her. She had never seen LeAnn this way. She made a point to talk to her after work. She walked into LeAnn's bedroom and noticed a suitcase sticking out from under the bed.

She could hear LeAnn in the bathroom, so she peaked inside and noticed clothes and money stashed inside. "Is she planning on going somewhere?" She wondered.

"What are you doing?" LeAnn asked as she walked out of the bathroom. "I saw the suitcase sticking out from under your bed. Where are you going?" Taylor asked.

"That's none of your business." LeAnn said as she bent down to push the suitcase under her bed further. "We used to tell each other everything. We were so close." Taylor said. "

"No, I used to tell you everything. You kept things from me." LeAnn stated.

"I never thought to talk to you about Joshua. I never expected that you would date his son. Joshua is my past and I wanted to keep him there." Taylor explained.

"Well, I wanted a future with Cameron, but thanks to you I'll never have that." LeAnn snapped.

"Let me help you fix it. I can talk to Blake. I know him better than anyone, after all he used to be my brother." Taylor begged.

"There's no fixing it. Everything is ruined now. There's no going back. What's done is done." LeAnn cried. She needed to get Taylor out of her room before she said too much. She couldn't tell her what Joshua did to her and that Cameron hates her now. She can't go back even if she wanted to.

"I need to be alone." LeAnn sobbed.

Taylor didn't know what more to say. She's given her so much space already, and LeAnn only seems to want more space. It broke her heart to see her hurting like this. She didn't know how to help her or what to say to earn her forgiveness other than to do what she asked. So, she left her bedroom. She let her be alone.

LeAnn wasn't the only one who wanted Joshua to suffer. Cameron was clearly done with him. He refused to talk to him which only made Joshua even more angry at LeAnn. Cameron hated him for stealing his girlfriend. He hated him for how he's treated his mother all these years.

His mom, Erin Haze was fed up with him too. She wanted a way out of their marriage. With the prenup she knew she'd walk away with nothing, unless she found some dirt on him to black male him into giving her what she wants.

Erin did some digging around and found his house by the golf course. He had kept so much hidden from her. He always took her for an idiot, but she was smarter than what he gave her credit for. She knew he had a bachelor pad, but she never knew where until now.

She had been in town the last two weeks living out of her car, so he wouldn't suspect her in the area. She watched his every move and memorized his schedule, so she knew when he wasn't at home.

He was so protective over his public image, so she knew if she found some dirt on him that would threaten his image, he would have no choice but to give her what she wants. She watched his every move. She saw where he hid his spare key down to the security code to his alarm system.

She had never been to this house, so she couldn't leave a trace of herself anywhere. She knew how shady he could be, and she wouldn't want him pin anything on her. She knew how ruthless he could be.

She snuck into his house while he was away. She carefully went through his drawers and looked underneath his mattress. She couldn't find anything. "His Trophy Room." She thought to herself. That's where he kept all the things he was proud of, and she was sure he thought of women he seduced as "trophies".

He kept that room locked, but with a credit card and paperclip she was able to jimmy the door open. In there she found numerous sex tapes. She then came across photos of Cameron having sex with a beautiful blonde girl. "What would he want with these?" She wondered.

The more she dug, the more she found. She recorded all the videos on her phone and took pictures of the photos he had of Cameron. Some videos stuck out the most. He had multiple videos of him having sex with the blonde girl from the photos with Cameron. At first, she thought the girl was just after their money, until she saw a video of Joshua raping her. She then looked closer at the other videos. She didn't look happy at all. She looked scared. Like she was being forced.

The videos made her even more angry. "That poor girl." She thought. She knew she needed to find out who this girl was and what were their intentions with her. She knew this wouldn't be enough to black male Joshua. There was a much deeper story here. She knew she needed to dig deeper.

She put everything back in it's place and locked the house back up and hurried out of there before Joshua came back home.

Over the next week LeAnn gave her future some serious thought. She didn't want to work with the family business anymore. She wanted a dream of her own. She didn't want this lifestyle anymore or be surrounded with rich and powerful people. She wanted to start over.

She always loved baking, but she's always been so busy helping with the family business that she never considered starting a career of her own. It was time to think about what she wanted for a change.

With her trust fund she could pay for culinary school and open her very own bakery. She could get out of this town and start over somewhere knew where no one knew who she was. She submitted her application to the finest culinary school in New York. This would be her ticket out of here.

"Taylor!"

LeAnn heard Blake scream from downstairs. She stood at the top of the stairwell to see what was going on. He looked angry and enraged!

"What the hell is this?" He yelled as he shoved the vanilla envelope at her. Taylors face turned ghost white as she looked inside the envelope.

"I can explain." She cried.

"I'm going to kill him!" Blake yelled.

"We love each other!" Taylor cried.

"You're eighteen! He's old enough to be your dad! What were you thinking for Christ sake!" He screamed.

He felt betrayed. Alex became his best friend after Jordan died. "Why the hell would he think this was okay?" He wondered. He was infuriated at the thought of his best friend, the man who once loved Jordan, screwing his eighteen-year old daughter.

He didn't give Taylor a chance to explain. He grabbed his keys and stormed out of the house.

"Joshua." LeAnn whispered. She knew he was behind this. This was a test. A test to show her what he's capable of. She knew she had to warn Taylor.

LeAnn went to Taylors bedroom to talk to her. She was trying to call Alex, but no answer. She knew he was at the gym.

She knew Blake was on his way there. They normally work out together. "Are you okay?" LeAnn asked.

"No. Someone sent Blake pictures of me and Alex having sex. Who would do that?" She cried. She suspected it was LeAnn who did it. She was the only one angry at her. She felt that Taylor ruined her relationship with Cameron and this was just her way of getting back at her.

"I trusted you." Taylor sobbed.

"What? It wasn't me!" LeAnn exclaimed.

"Who else would do this to me? No one knows about us but you!" Taylor cried.

LeAnn wanted to tell her. She even considered telling her, but then everyone would know her secrets and her photos would end up on the internet. She didn't know what to tell her or how to get her to believe her without telling the truth.

"I swear on my life is wasn't me. I would never do that to you, no matter how angry I am." LeAnn pleaded.

"Get out!" Taylor screamed.

"Taylor please, you have to believe me! Someone else is behind this!" LeAnn cried.

"Who?" Taylor asked.

LeAnn was terrified. Her body was trembling, but she had no choice but to tell her. It was only a matter of time before Joshua did the same thing to her.

"Joshua Haze." LeAnn confessed.

Chapter 16

Blake rushed into the gym like a raging storm. He saw Alex bench pressing with his spotter. He pushed him out of the way and pushed the bar of weights down on Alex. Alex struggled for a moment to push the bar back up and with one gust of adrenaline he pushed the bar off him causing Blake to fall back.

Alex immediately jumped to his feet, but Blake didn't hesitate. He charged at Alex knocking him down to the floor and began punching him. The men at the gym pulled Blake off him.

"You're supposed to be my friend! I trusted you!" Blake yelled.

Alex didn't bother asking him what this was about. He already knew. "Taylor must have told him." He thought. "Blake let me explain." Alex said.

"Explain what? How you pretend to be my friend while you're screwing my daughter!" Blake screamed.

"I'll tell you everything, but you need to calm down." Alex said.

"Calm down! She's eighteen-years old Alex! She's practically a child! She's a teenager!" Blake screamed at the top of his lungs.

"She's not who you think she is Blake. She's Jordan." Alex confessed.

"You are sick and twisted. You need psychiatric help!" Blake yelled. He could believe that Alex would think she was Jordan unless he was mentally unstable.

He spent so many years dealing with his own grief that he completely ignored the signs of the perverted monster that grief was turning Alex into. Grief made him obsessive. Taylor looked so much like Jordan that Blake believed Alex came up with some twisted fantasy in his head.

"You both need to leave!" The gym manager yelled sternly.

"You stay the hell away from my family or I'll kill you." Blake warned.

Over the next couple of days Blake was very quiet. Taylor noticed that he had been giving her the silent treatment. He made small talk with everyone else at the dinner table except her, and every time she tried to talk to him he had something more important to do.

This hurt her so deeply. She wanted Blake to know who she was and believe her. He had his sister back this whole time and never knew it. Before she could try to mend things with Blake, she had to know what was going on with LeAnn. "Why would LeAnn think Joshua was behind this? What does she know that I don't?" She wondered.

With everything that was going on, she never thought to ask her, why she thought it was him. It was time for LeAnn to tell her everything she knows.

She needed time to think. How was she going to find out the truth about what LeAnn was hiding? LeAnn hasn't been wanting to tell her things lately, but this is important. She needed to get out of the house to clear her head before she talked to LeAnn.

She went to the park to clear her head. She wished she could talk to Alex. He always had the best advice. She waked around staring at the necklace he had given her. "Life is like a changing season." Whatever LeAnn was hiding, she knew they could get through it together. But, she had to get her to be honest with her first.

She knew what she had to do. LeAnn doesn't do well under pressure. Just then she knew exactly what to say to her. She was going to get to the bottom of this.

When she came back home, she went upstairs to LeAnn's bedroom to bombard her with questions. She had to get her to talk.

"Why do you think Joshua is behind this?" Taylor asked.

"It's just a hunch. He bought those photos of you at the art gallery. I think he's obsessed with you." LeAnn lied.

Taylor didn't believe that. She knew there was more to the story. She's known Joshua for a long time and that doesn't make any sense.

"Tell me the truth." Taylor said.

"I am telling you the truth. You look a lot like Jordan and I think he's still in love with Jordan." LeAnn said.

"I've known Joshua a long time, and I can tell you for a fact that he never loved Jordan. I know there's more to the story LeAnn, and I'm not afraid to dig deep. Don't lie to me." Taylor warned.

LeAnn felt her heart race. It was pounding so hard like it was going to explode inside her chest. Sweat began to drip from her forehead. Taylor could see that she was nervous. LeAnn's breath became shallow and shaky.

She knew that if she told her the truth, things were going to get messier. Their family's reputation would be at risk. They could lose everything if those photos ended up on the internet. She knew Taylor was serious about digging around. She'd end up finding out what was going on and it could ruin everything. Then Taylor would hate her for lying.

She had no choice. She had to confess. Even if it destroyed them.

"Okay, sit down. I'll tell you everything." LeAnn said.

LeAnn was so scared to tell her, but she knew she had to. Taylor knew him better than anyone and might know what to do.

"I continued to see Cameron after dad told me not to. We were going to figure out a way to win dads approval. Joshua knew that my dad wouldn't allow Cameron and I to see each other anymore because Cameron told him. Joshua hired someone to follow us and take pictures. Then he invited me to lunch at his house and confronted me with the pictures. He threatened to send them to my dad if I didn't do what he wanted. He said he'd give me one picture back every time I had sex with him. So, I did. Then one day Cameron walked in on us. He wouldn't even let me explain myself. I told Joshua I was done and that I didn't care if he sent those pictures. He then threatened to put them on the internet. He slapped me and forced me inside and..." LeAnn choked up and began sobbing hysterically.

"He raped you." Taylor finished for her. LeAnn nodded her head yes.

"I think these pictures of you are his way of showing me what he's capable of. He's trying to scare me to get what he wants. I've been ignoring his text messages. I'm sure he's quite angry about that. I have to get out of here." LeAnn cried.

"You have to go to the police and tell them what happened." Taylor encouraged.

"I can't. I threw away the pictures he gave me, and I deleted the text messages he sent. They wouldn't believe me. I have no proof." LeAnn said.

Taylor was infuriated. "How can she be so stupid? Why would you delete the only proof you have? Did she really delete those messages or is she just afraid of hurting Cameron? Or, is she in fact that terrified of Joshua? She should have never let it get this far... but how could she have stopped it? She's so young and Joshua has a way of getting what he wants. Fear can make a young vulnerable girl do things she normally wouldn't. She's not thinking clearly." Taylor thought.

"You didn't do anything wrong. This wasn't your fault. Joshua is a scum bag and I should have warned you a long time ago about him." Taylor said.

She knew Joshua was a cheater, but never expected him to be a rapist too. She knew he's get girls drunk and possibly slip drugs in their drink and take advantage of them, but to black male and rape his sister was a whole other level of low. She wanted him to pay for what he has done.

She knew LeAnn wouldn't tell Cameron the truth, but someone had to. He needed to know. LeAnn shouldn't have to pay the price for what Joshua did to her. Taylor was determined to ruin his life.

The problems of her own would have to wait. She needed to protect LeAnn at all cost. She needed to save her sister from anything else Joshua had in store for her, including public humiliation.

Taylor waited until she was alone to call Jack. She needed to gather proof. Jack was more than willing to spy on Joshua and find out how to get into his house and figure out the times that he wouldn't be at home.

With Jacks help she was able to find out where he hid his spare key and the security code to his house. Jack watched him for a week and learned the times he's be gone.

"You know I'd do anything for you, but what is this about?" Jack asked.

Taylor wanted to keep LeAnn's secret. So, she didn't go into too much detail.

"He's trying to black male my family, and I can't go into detail without deceiving someone I love." Taylor said.

Jack understood and didn't ask anymore questions. He handed over all the information he had on Joshua. Taylor didn't hesitate. As soon as Joshua left his house she went inside to snoop around.

Taylor couldn't believe what she found. Not only did she find the pictures, but she also found videos of Joshua and LeAnn having sex, including the rape video.

"LeAnn never mentioned videos." Taylor thought. She didn't notice any cameras in his house. "He must have a camera hidden in his bedroom." She thought. She didn't have time to look. She knew Joshua would be back any minute.

She wondered if she should tell LeAnn about the videos. She took the pictures and the videos of LeAnn. Although she noticed videos of other women, she left those ones where they were. She just hoped he wouldn't notice the videos of LeAnn were gone.

On her way out, she noticed the photos of her from Jacks art show that Joshua purchased. Out of anger she took those too. She didn't want him to have anything that had to do with her family.

She wore gloves just in case he noticed things missing and called the cops to report a robbery. But then again, why would he? A rape video was stolen. He'd be stupid to call the cops.

When she got home she played the videos in her bedroom and recorded the rape video on her phone. She sent the video to Cameron and texted, "LeAnn is innocent in all of this. You need to know what kind of man your father is."

She didn't think twice about sending it. She knew it wasn't her story to tell, but she was so angry. She needed to tell LeAnn about the videos. She had the proof she needed to turn him into the cops.

When she brought the evidence to LeAnn, she was hesitant. "I can't." LeAnn said.

"Why? You said you needed proof!" Taylor argued.

"You broke into his house. You could go to jail too!" LeAnn exclaimed.

"I don't care! I'll go to jail if that means that you get justice for what he did!" Taylor yelled.

"He's a celebrity! If I go to the cop's then everyone in the world will know what happened! That's just as bad as those photos going on the internet. I don't want anyone to know!" LeAnn cried.

Taylor felt frustrated. She didn't know what else to do or how to help LeAnn.

"It might help other women to come forward. You're probably not the only one he did this too." Taylor said. She knew she wasn't the only one. She saw the other videos but didn't want to upset LeAnn anymore by telling her.

"No. I'm not telling anyone. No one can find out about this. I got accepted into culinary school in New York. I'm going to move and leave this whole mess behind me." LeAnn said.

"Running won't make this go away." Taylor said.

"That's why I'm not coming back. I'm leaving for good." LeAnn confessed.

"That would devastate everyone if you never came back. You have to stay and fight this." Taylor argued.

"I said no. You have to destroy the pictures and videos." LeAnn ordered.

A part of LeAnn felt free. Joshua no longer had those pictures or videos in his possession. She had nothing holding her back now. She could leave with out the fear of repercussion. She just needed to leave as soon as possible before he noticed those pictures and videos were gone.

She had no idea he was recording them having sex. She wondered what his intentions were for those videos. She knew he couldn't be trusted. He was all kinds of shady. "Thank God no one else knows and that Taylor will keep this a secret." LeAnn thought.

Chapter 17

"I'm going to kill him." Cameron texted Taylor.

"Don't say or do anything. LeAnn doesn't know that I told you. If Joshua suspects that you know, there's no telling what he'll do to LeAnn." Taylor texted back.

"So, I'm supposed to just sit back and do nothing? My father RAPED MY GIRLFRIEND!" Cameron texted.

"Don't do anything stupid. We have, to talk LeAnn into going to the police. That's the smart thing to do." Taylor texted.

The guilt was tearing her apart. She should have never told Cameron or sent that video. If LeAnn found out, she would never forgive her, and they were finally getting along again.

Alex hasn't been responding to her calls or text messages. She needed his advice on what to do. Since he wouldn't respond to her, she drove to his house and knocked on his door.

"What are you doing here? Your dad will kill me if he finds out you're here." Alex warned.

"This isn't about us. I need your advice." Taylor said.

"Then you should ask your parents for advice, not me." Alex said.

"Joshua Haze raped LeAnn." Taylor blurted out.

"What? She needs to go to the police." Alex said.

"She won't. She doesn't want anyone to know. I don't know what to do." Taylor said.

"Well, technically you're her aunt. So, you have, to protect her. You have, to ask yourself what Jordan would do. Jordan would tell her father. She would protect her at all cost." Alex advised.

"You're right... I miss you Alex." Taylor said.

"I miss you too, but we hurt your dad. Blake will never forgive me. This just wasn't meant to be. I want you to live your life out as Taylor. Forget who Jordan was. Fall in love again, travel, and make new memories. Experience all that life has to offer you. I'll never stop loving you." Alex said.

She knew he was right, but all she wanted was to be with him. "Why can't we run away like LeAnn?" She wondered. But, she knew why. It wasn't the adult thing to do. It would only hurt her family more.

It broke her heart at the thought of letting him go. But, she had to make sure that LeAnn was safe first and then mend her relationship with Blake.

Within a week her whole family took a trip to New York to help LeAnn move into her new apartment. While Blake and Brit were downstairs getting the last two boxes, Taylor found this the perfect time to have a heart to heart talk with LeAnn.

"This is your fresh start. Don't be nervous." Taylor said.

"I'm more excited than nervous. Maybe a little nervous." LeAnn laughed.

"Don't walk in dark alleys. Don't venture too far out into the city and get lost. If you're ever unsure about a stranger approaching you just pepper spray them." Taylor said as she handed her pepper spray to put on her key chain.

"You worry too much. I'll be fine." LeAnn assured her.

"I know you will. You're strong. I just don't want anything bad to happen to you." Taylor said.

"It won't. I'll be careful. The bad stuff is behind me now." LeAnn said.

Taylor hugged her so tight. "You've been the best sister anyone could ask for. I'll come visit you often. Hell, maybe I'll eventually move to the big city with you." Taylor said.

"I would love that. New York is so pretty in the fall. I can't wait to see it when it snows." LeAnn said.

Golf season was almost over. Soon Joshua would be on a plane out of here and their life could get back to normal. Well. Almost normal. With LeAnn gone and Blake still giving Taylor the silent treatment, she knew life would be lonely.

Maybe she should move to New York with LeAnn once things settle back home. Lord knows she needed a fresh start too.

When they got back home, Taylor went to have lunch with her friends. She told them her plans about enrolling into college and moving to New York in a few months. Jack and Alison said they applied to colleges there already and would move with her.

She needed this. She needed to adapt to her life as Taylor. Move to a new city and make new memories. This is what Alex wanted for her. She was ready to start fresh. Nothing was going to hold her back. At least that's what she thought until the police showed up at her door one morning.

"Did Cameron take that video to the police?" She wondered. If so, she knew things were about to get real ugly. When the police left she went downstairs to ask Blake what that was about.

"Why were the police here?" She asked.

Blake looked like he had seen a ghost. "Joshua Haze was found murdered in his home." He said.

Taylor began to panic on the inside. Her heart began to race, and the palms of her hands began to sweat. "Who were the suspects?" She wondered. She had videos of LeAnn being raped and photos of LeAnn and Cameron having sex. What if the cops found all this evidence? She never destroyed them like LeAnn told her too.

"Did Cameron kill him?" She wondered. She remembered she sent him the rape video. "Or was LeAnn moving to New York for an alibi for a crime she was plotting?" She wondered. Who knows who else Cameron showed the video to. He wanted to win Blakes approval. Was this how? Was Blake in on it?

Things were about to get messy, and soon everyone would find out the raw truth.